Quentin Blake

COCKATOOS

JONATHAN CAPE
LONDON

to my friends in France

Copyright © Quentin Blake 1992
Reprinted 1992, 1993, 1995, 1998
Jonathan Cape Ltd, 20 Vauxhall Bridge Road, London SW1V 2SA
A CIP catalogue record is available from the British Library
ISBN 0 224 03115 5
Printed in China

Professor Dupont had ten cockatoos.
He was very proud of them.

Every morning he jumped out of bed.

He took a shower and
he cleaned his teeth,

as he always did.

He got dressed and he tied his tie,
as he always did.

He adjusted his spectacles,
as he always did.

And he went downstairs.

He went into the conservatory.
There were all his cockatoos;
                    every single one.

Professor Dupont threw wide his arms.
He said: "Good morning,
                    my fine feathered friends!"

Every morning he said the same thing.
The day came when the cockatoos thought they would go
mad if they had to listen to the same words once again.

They decided to have some sport with Professor Dupont.
One after another they escaped through a broken pane of
glass they had discovered in a corner of the conservatory.

Next morning Professor Dupont came into the
conservatory and threw wide his arms.
There was not a cockatoo in sight.

Where could all the cockatoos have got to?

Professor Dupont went into the dining-room.
They weren't there.

He went to look in the kitchen.
Hortense the cook was there,
boiling an egg for his breakfast,
but there weren't any cockatoos.

He went to look in the bedroom.
They weren't there.

He looked in the bathroom.
They weren't there.

He looked in the lavatory.
They weren't there.

He climbed a ladder
        and flashed his torch around the attic.
            They weren't there.

He even climbed up to the roof.
But they weren't there.

Professor Dupont went to look in the garage.
His car was there,
but there weren't any cockatoos.

He went down into the cellar; but he couldn't see any cockatoos there, either.

Professor Dupont was at his wit's end.
He couldn't find his cockatoos anywhere.
Where could they possibly have got to?

Professor Dupont spent a restless night.

The next morning he jumped out of bed.
He took a shower and he cleaned his teeth,
as he always did.

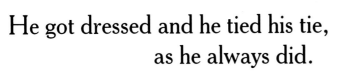

He got dressed and he tied his tie,
as he always did.

He adjusted his spectacles,
as he always did.

And he went downstairs.

Professor Dupont went into the conservatory.
There were all his cockatoos, where they
always were – every single one!

Professor Dupont threw wide his arms.
He said: "Good morning,
my fine feathered friends!"

Some people never learn.